Deep-Sea Dreams

FINDDORY7373

Code is valid for your ebook and may be
redeemed through the Disney Story Central app
on the App Store. Content subject to availability.
Parent permission required.
Code expires on December 31, 2019.

Bath · New York · Cologne · Melbourne · Delhi
Hong Kong · Shenzhen · Singapore · Amsterdam

"Hi, I'm Dory! I suffer from short-term memory loss."
Dory is a baby blue tang who forgets things easily.

Jenny and Charlie are Dory's parents. They love their daughter and do their best to protect her.

One day, Dory gets separated from her parents.
She asks other fish for help, but they swim away.

Dory grows up into a happy, friendly fish.
After a while, she forgets what she was looking for
and where she came from.

One day, Dory meets a fish called Marlin.
He's looking for his son, Nemo. Nemo is lost, too!

Marlin is a clownfish. Dory helps him find his son.
He is very happy when they are reunited.

Nemo lives with his dad in an anemone. He has lots of energy and is very curious about the world.

Marlin loves his son so much, he can be
a little bit overprotective sometimes.

Marlin and Nemo are just like family to Dory.
She even lives next door to them.

Dory and Marlin swim to school with Nemo,
but Marlin worries that Dory will forget
where she is going and get lost.

Mr. Ray is Nemo's teacher—and the school bus!
He carries all the children to school on his back.

Dory is Mr. Ray's assistant for the day, but she's not very good at teaching. Today's lesson is about migration.

A student asks Dory where her real home is.
Dory can't remember.

Mr. Ray brings the class on a field trip to the coral reef.
He sings a song about migration, and Dory joins in.

Here come the migrating stingrays!
Their flapping wings create a strong current.

Dory gets too close to the stingray migration.
She gets pulled into the current and knocked out!

When Dory wakes up, she thinks she remembers
something important . . . but she's not sure what it is.

**Marlin is worried about Dory.
He brings her home.**

The next morning, Dory knows what she remembered.
She has a family in California!

Dory, Marlin, and Nemo are going to California with some help from Crush and Squirt.

Dory tells Crush that she is looking for her parents. Crush says that he can give them a ride on his shell.

The current makes Marlin seasick!

They finally arrive in California. Dory, Marlin, and Nemo meet a group of hermit crabs with very funny shells.

Dory remembers asking the hermit crabs for help when she was a baby. They weren't very nice.

Marlin tries to talk to the crabs, but they won't answer.

They accidentally wake a giant squid.
He's angry!

The giant squid chases them through the shipping lanes!
Dory, Marlin, and Nemo get caught in plastic rings.

Dory swims away as fast as she can,
but she is still caught in the plastic rings.

Dory swims to the surface. A person in a boat lifts her out of the water and takes her to the Marine Life Institute—the MLI.

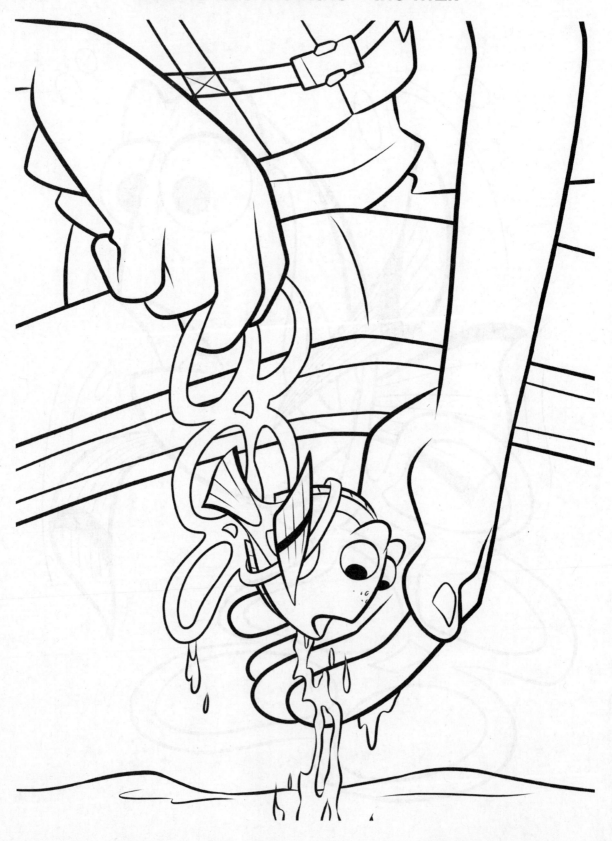

Dory realizes that the MLI is where she is from!
She is put in a tank and given a special tag.

Hank is an octopus, but he has only seven tentacles.
That makes him a septopus!

Hank wants Dory's tag so he can move to an aquarium in Cleveland. Dory wants him to help her find her parents.

Hank reluctantly agrees to help Dory
in exchange for her tag.

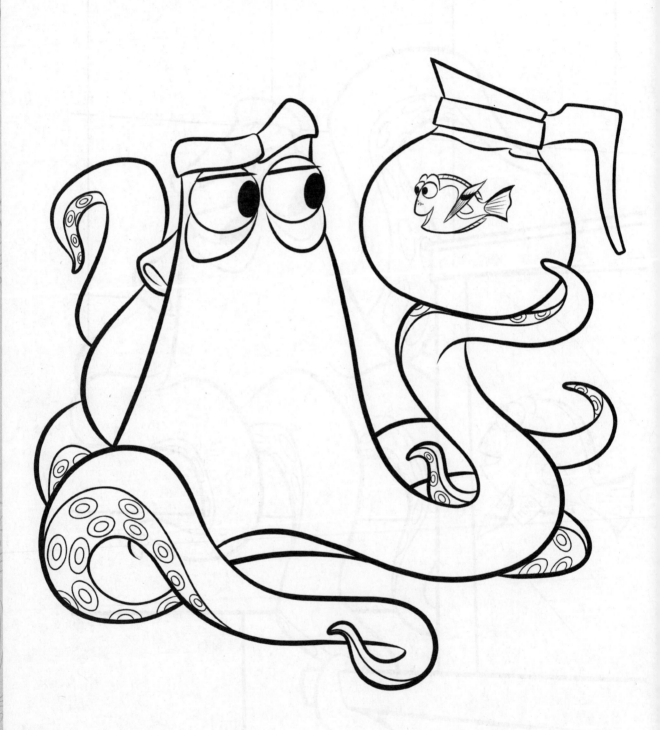

Dory looks at a map of the MLI and tries
to remember where her parents live. . . .

Dory has a flashback! She remembers collecting shells with her parents when she was a baby.

Hank and Dory hide from an MLI worker who walks past.
Hank is an expert at camouflage.

Dory sees a bucket with "DESTINY" written on it.
She thinks it might lead to her parents, so she jumps into it.

The worker takes the bucket to Destiny the whale shark!
She lives in the MLI because she can't see very well.

Dory jumps into Destiny's tank.
She helps Destiny swim straight.

Destiny realizes that she and Dory were friends when they were young. Destiny taught Dory to speak whale!

Bailey is a beluga whale. He is Destiny's neighbor. He is in the MLI because he can't use his special echolocation skill to see things that are far away.

Destiny tells Dory that she can get to her home in the
Open Ocean exhibit by swimming through the pipes.
Dory is scared that she will get lost.

Becky is a loon. She can help Marlin and Nemo get into the MLI to find Dory.

Becky likes Marlin a lot!

Fluke and Rudder are a pair of very lazy sea lions.
They are going to help Marlin and Nemo get into the MLI.

Gerald is also a sea lion.
He likes to carry a pail in his mouth!

Fluke and Rudder offer to share their rock
with Gerald if he will let them use his pail.

Becky scoops Marlin and Nemo up in the pail and flies toward the MLI.

**Destiny causes a splash in her pool
to help her friends escape.**

Hank finds a way for them to get to the Open Ocean exhibit—in a stroller! Dory steers while Hank drives.

Becky has left Marlin and Nemo in a tree. They're stuck!
They try to find a way down.

Becky forgets all about Marlin and Nemo
when she sees some popcorn.

Dory and Hank pass the sea otter exhibit.
They're so cute and cuddly!

Dory and Hank have fallen into the touch pool
and they can't get out.

Hank is so scared that he inks in the
touch pool and turns the water black.

Dory remembers her parents teaching
her the "Just Keep Swimming" song.
She and Hank need to just keep swimming!

Dory and Hank finally escape.
They make a great team!

Hank and Dory finally reach the Open Ocean exhibit.
"Home," Dory says, happily.

Marlin and Nemo finally get out of the tree.
They fall into a tank full of robot fish!

Hank and Dory barely escape getting caught.
They're nearly there, and Dory is excited.

Hank climbs across the scaffolding to the Open Ocean exhibit. Dory can't wait to be reunited with her family.

Marlin and Nemo are still stuck in the fish tank.
"What would Dory do?" asks Nemo.

Marlin and Nemo finally escape from the tank.

They land in a tidal pool. They keep thinking like Dory, and get a little bit closer to finding her.

They meet a loudmouthed clam who likes to talk a lot.
"What would Dory do?" Marlin asks Nemo.

Hank finally gets Dory close to home.
Dory gives her tag to Hank so he can go to Cleveland.

Dory swims into the Open Ocean exhibit.

Dory sees a trail of shells.
They seem familiar. . . .

Dory finds her childhood home . . . but there's no one there.

Dory suddenly remembers being pulled away into the pipes when she was young. That's how she got lost!

Dory bravely swims into the pipes to find her parents, but she forgets the way and gets lost.

Dory speaks to Destiny in whale through the pipes. She asks for help.

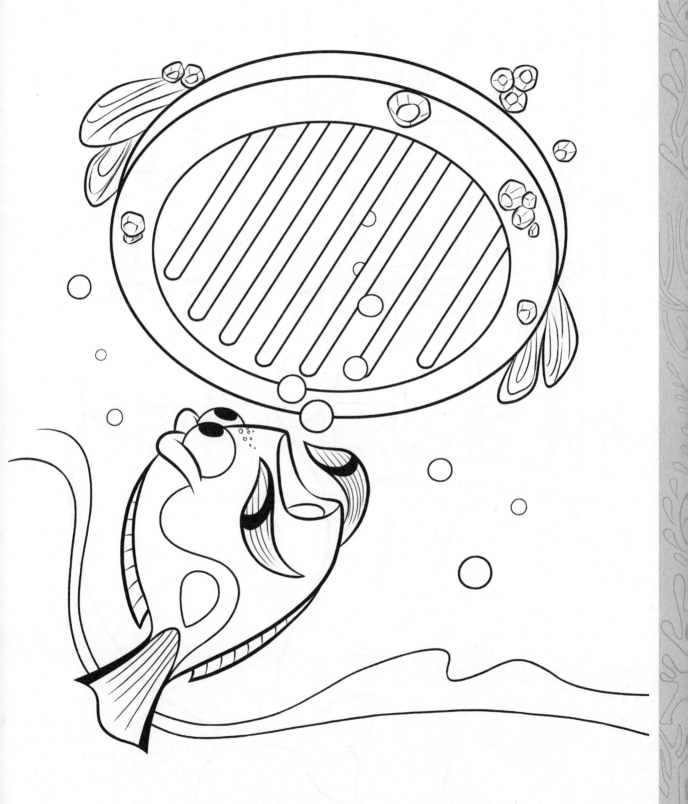

Bailey remembers how to use his echolocation so he can help Dory find her way through the pipes.

Dory finds Marlin and Nemo!
They tell her that they have come to help her.

Hank is ready to go to Cleveland, when he sees Dory with Marlin and Nemo in Quarantine.

Dory hopes that she will find her parents
in the tank of blue tangs.

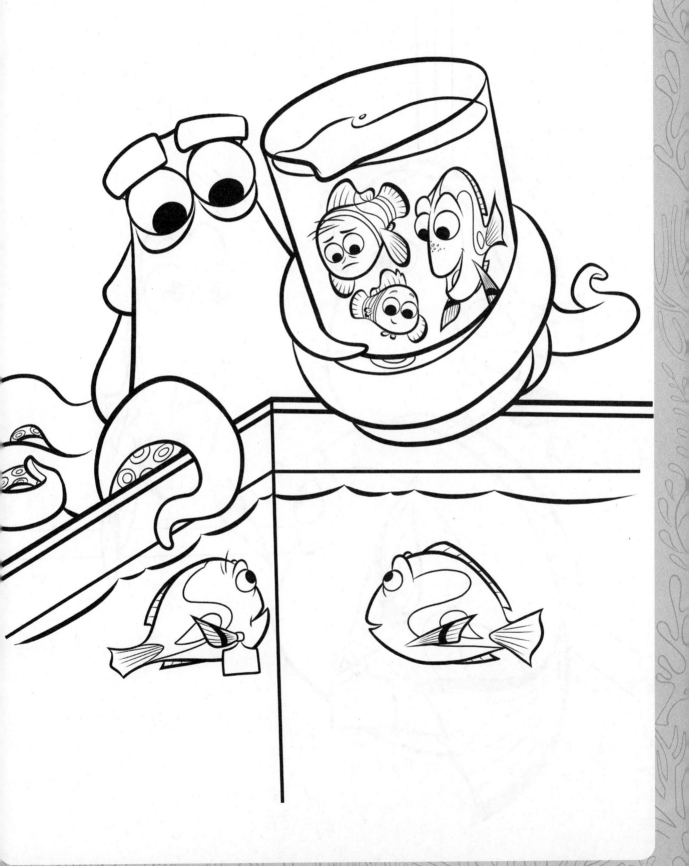

But Dory's parents aren't there. The blue tangs tell her that they left a long time ago. Dory is upset.

When Hank is startled, Dory flies through the air and slips down a drain that leads to the ocean.

Marlin, Nemo, and Hank are loaded onto the transport truck. They're headed to Cleveland!

The drain leads Dory into the open ocean.
She doesn't know which way to go.
She asks herself, "What would Dory do?"

Dory sees paths made of shells. They seem familiar.
She decides to follow them.

Dory is reunited with her parents! They made the shell paths so she would find them. They've been waiting for her for a long time, and they are very happy to see her.

Dory needs to save Marlin and Nemo.
She calls on Bailey and Destiny for help.
They leap out of their pools and into the ocean.

Bailey uses his echolocation again to find
the truck carrying Marlin and Nemo.
The group swims off to rescue them!

The sea otters help Dory stop the truck
with a big cuddle party.

Dory reaches Marlin and Nemo!

Becky helps save Marlin and Nemo,
but Dory is left behind!

Dory's parents finally meet Marlin and Nemo.
They like them right away!

Hank takes action to stop the truck!

Hank drives while Dory directs him,
just like they did before.

"Follow the seagulls!" Dory says. She knows
they will lead them back to the sea.

Hank and Dory drive the truck into the ocean!

Dory goes home with her family and all her new friends.

Hank is the new substitute teacher.
Bailey and Destiny are his assistants.

**Dory's family is finally complete.
She couldn't be happier.**